The Mayflies

Sara Veglahn

DZANC
BOOKS

5220 Dexter Ann Arbor Rd.
Ann Arbor, MI 48103
www.dzancbooks.org

The Mayflies

Copyright © 2014, text by Sara Veglahn.

Published 2014 by Dzanc Books
ISBN: 978-1938103773
First edition:

This project is supported in part by the National Endowment
for the Arts and the MCACA.

Printed in the United States of America

Prologue

IN THE BEGINNING, THERE WAS WATER. Just a trickle, nothing more. Soon rain and more rain, and later: a flood. In time, the water shifted from a small still pool and embraced gravity. It moved in a line over rocks and trees and cities and towns. A whole world covered in water. A whole world outside the water.

The river gained speed and coursed through the valley it had made. What started as a clear stream merged into something muddy and full of catfish and mayflies and other things that fell and disappeared into the dark water.

In the beginning, a mayfly has no wings. She lies buried until it is time to emerge. Once she reaches the surface and removes herself from the mud, she is altered.

In dreams, I walk through mud. I fall into it and feel changed. My ladies are always there, as they are always here with me now.

I began as a girl. She began as me.

I pull myself up and out and stand with water streaming from my limbs and hair. I am a fountain. The ancient story of girls who followed each other one by one into the river and never came back is repeated until the story becomes a story of only one girl who follows nothing and goes into the river alone.

This is how that story goes:

I walk through the streets at dawn. A thick fog hovers here and there.

At dawn, I am out on the street, my pace steady, my shoes sharp clacking on the pavement. There is no one else.

The river comes into view only as I reach it. It's summer, and there's a damp heat rising from the patch of grass where I now stand. The water laps against the heavy black rocks. It is nearly time for the mayfly hatching.

Until I reach it, the river is invisible.

She is here and I am her.

My wings emerge damp and fragile.

She carries herself down to the water.

My captors, my saviors, myself.

The world outside.

Nothing changes.

It is unclear where the water ends when everything is water.

Her outline makes a shadow against the wall. It moves with the cool breeze that comes in through the window. A situation of disappearance. No one knows where she's gone and she isn't sure either. Solid ground, yes, but slippery and moveable. She is scattered across the floor.

I see her there and begin to gather the fragments.

I am here.

Can you see?

Look into the water. My face makes many faces.

And there is this day, right now.

There is the day before and the day to come.

There is each day.

The Mayflies

EACH DAY WE PULL OURSELVES OUT OF THE RIVER. The streets and sidewalks are marked with a trail of our damp footprints, yet we are nowhere to be found. We sing all of the old songs, march in a line like children. At night, in summer, our steam rises. You believe you see a hand emerge from the water, a dark soaked head of hair that turns toward you. You think you see us in windows and doorways, in dining halls and tea rooms. We are there, beside you but we are not there. We are there beside you and we are there and not. We are always there beside you.

A new moon. The kind seen in daytime. A chance of snow or freezing rain. The heat wave was predicted to last several more weeks, and the newly hatched mayflies covered everything. In meadows, crickets formed their songs. In the songs, a train from far away, an ear pressed to the rails. Something sloshing. All of the ladies in their Egyptian costumes were standing on the balustrades, their arms and hands making sharp angles. Hundreds of ladies and hundreds of angles.

I moved through corridors. Blood to blood. No light. Lost.

A motorcycle or car raced to where someone would pull me out, sticky and wet. A bus or train was racing there, where someone, I don't know who, pulled me out. I was no longer attached to my mother. I was no longer attached to my father.

Before everything, there are first things. Small high window views. Her little prison when she was small and waiting. She saw everything that she saw. A mistake in wanting. Everyone waving where she could monster. Throw this mean over the fence. And now flung or thinking so. She was waked.

Try to catch her. There, in the meadow. She traverses the region of ripples. She is transparent and obvious as she flies. Unused to such movement, she grows tired. There is a summer inside her summer. She returns to mud and is troubled. She waits. It is morning again and she is alone with the light. Three come to greet her. She sees them standing above. Her tiny eyes are confused by their faces reflected in the water.

In the first dream I remember, I walk back and forth on a red footbridge and stop to watch the rushing water. It is like the water that comes out from the side of a dam. It is very cold and the water is several shades of gray. There's an airplane in the sky writing a message in smoke that I cannot read. I am alone in a field. It is winter but almost spring and very muddy. I don't like walking in the mud. I fall down into something soft, like feathers. I can't remember anything more from this first dream.

In the middle of nowhere (outside the outside world)

A mother walks into the steam of a steam train and disappears

(once upon a time)

Two sisters run to the tracks they put their ears to the rails

A door opens to a door and to another

Everything river-colored

Furrowed fields

To get to the river and the ghost

They must run a long way

She is a fly in the water

(some girls can jump through fire)

One girl decides to leave in the night

The constant agitation of the river bottom

She goes to see her ghost

When he comes to her she is unafraid

"Tell me what happened"

A man walks in to a river…

There is the whistle and smoke of a train

They stand as it passes

They yell into the water

The first time I speak to a ghost I don't realize it's not a real person. I sit in a green chair and look out the window at the wind blowing the trees so hard I think they'll break. I've been looking out this window in my apartment for a long time.

My back is to the door of the room in which I sit and that is when I hear a low voice. The voice says my full name. I think the voice belongs to a neighbor or to someone delivering a package. I say, "Yes? What is it? Are you downstairs? I'm coming right down."

I reach the front door and see no one. I look all around, up and down the street. I go back inside and look in every room, every closet, every dark corner. I am not afraid. I don't hear the voice again.

Below the surface. The burden of air and taking it in. I've buried myself deep in mud and silt. My ladies are looking for me, I know. They will find me soon enough, but how will I appear?

She is here too. She sits folded into the sediment. We hold hands and look to the sky that wavers in the wake.

The first stage of life is water through the body. Her body is water. It is water, air, and salt. She is there in the mud. In mud she lies in wait. There is a transformation. Stones and vegetation, thorax and wings. Abdomen and legs, tail and gills. Each stage presents a great vulnerability. She flies and everything empties out. She burrows and becomes different. She lets go her anchor, lets the water go. She floats to the surface.

One year, early in adulthood, I went to live alone on an island off the coast of Scandinavia. The rocks were hard and black and it rained almost every day. The house had many windows and sheer draperies. There was always a breeze flowing through the place putting everything into motion. My ladies either lounged in the sun or searched the beach for small shells. A young woman who looked like me came once a week with supplies. One time she told me everything about her life. I listened but she grew frustrated by my silence. Then she tried to become me and I tried to become her. We tried to switch.

Later, when I was dying, I saw nothing but the ceiling of my room, the arcs of plaster hanging by threads, the plaster angels losing their faces. I was both silent and could not stop speaking. I said things like, "A long road down to the valley", and, "There is nothing but the shape of your hands to call you back, to tell you what you must do." My ladies continued on. They massaged my arms with fragrant oils, they sang low clear songs.

When I look at my hands I think, *These are not mine. This is not me.*

Mud and insects and we went walking there right down in it, fish smell, dead fish, mud and insects, we went there walking at night in the summer it was different than in winter, it never froze really, there was a slime that covered you if you submerged yourself and you couldn't get the smell out, it was more than mud or insects, or fish smell, dead fish, it was rotten, the impossibility of really reaching the bottom because the bottom was so deep with mud whatever was down there something ancient like the catfish that hovered slowly suspended moving barely their scales like armor, their ancient bodies a call to a past we weren't a part of, this smell, it got into everything.

She spent days alone in the city, where she wandered back and forth between the apartment she rented downtown and the bridge with its red neon sign advertising beer and its blue neon sign advertising flour. It was a time of collecting things.

She picked up everything she found. Someone's lost shopping list or coat button. A shard of green glass worn smooth by traffic. Once, a fifty dollar bill dropped outside the museum. She looked around for someone looking around for lost money, but when no one appeared, she slipped it into her mitten and kept it folded against her palm.

Soft snow grabbed her hair and coat. Her boots on the salted sidewalk made a noise like chewing. She gazed at her apartment building from across the street. It looked both warm and hollow. She crossed the street and climbed the stairs to the door. Her key did not fit into the lock. She tried it the other way and it still didn't work. She tried a different key and it didn't work either. She tried every key she had. It was dark and cold and getting colder. She sat on the stairs and examined her keys. They seemed familiar. Nothing was different. She tried again—each key right-side up and upside down. Something must have happened. She turned to the buzzers on the wall to try to call someone, anyone, to let her in. As she scanned the names for a familiar name, she saw that her name was not among them. A sound like waves sloshed through her. She returned to the street and saw that it was not her building. She was on the wrong street. She had been so sure that this was where she lived.

I have a dream in which a horse is stolen by horse thieves. I am supposed to ride this horse, but when I come back from getting ready to do so, the horse has been stolen and the thieves are waiting for me too.

It didn't stop raining for days. The water kept rising. We didn't know what to do except wait for it to stop. The road became a river. The water moved so fast you would be carried away if you fell into it. An expanse of water larger than the valley it filled. Bursting its banks. Such escapes—away from rivers and the language of rivers. To seek something soft like mud or feathers. You wouldn't be found. The water bursting its banks.

When I died, the sun shone strong. A clear day without much breeze. All the traffic was stopped on the bridge and no one was in any hurry. Many people stood outside of their cars, reading the paper and waiting to go. Everyone in their summer clothes, everyone alive.

The streets where I died were narrow with shadow. The shadows expanded past the corner store. I would walk through days inhaling and exhaling. I would have to close the blinds to the glare. Everything I loved was placed into boxes. Everything I had was packed away.

I gazed long at the soft sun. I was down.

When the great wave burst through me, I was stranded. Drowning on concrete, the sidewalk clanging with bells, I opened the door and had faith in symmetry. What did I know? My ladies redoubled. They ate red popsicles and drooled the juice down. They imitated each other's rhythm, seeming sorry, all of them saying, "Run along now, run along."

One woman saw a horse in human flesh, descending on a hammock through the air, and as it neared her house it was metamorphosed into a man, and this man approached her door and threw something at her that seemed to be rubber but turned into great bees.

Another was lost in a vast swimming pool where she found she could breathe the water, that it was better than breathing air. Once she finally was able to emerge from the pool, she was transported to a large room filled with sugar. Everything was made from it: the furniture, the light fixtures, the paintings on the wall. The room seemed prepared for a great banquet and there was a long table filled with food. The food was made from either sugar or salt molded into the shapes of fruits and meats. It seemed she was sent there to figure out which was which.

"But is that all you can remember?" the ladies asked. They sat in a row, sequined. They stared at her with their beautiful eyes, blinking flashes of blue and green and purple.

"Every city has a list of the presidents that moves from north to south or east to west," she said. "It's chilling, this kind of organization."

Her ladies stared. They were smiling now. They said, "Go on."

"Between the small house and the big house there was a tall cement wall, and an alleyway with other houses raised like lanterns. I ran along the ledges toward the alleys up to the lantern houses and back down again. There was a brewery, which was like its own city, and the bakery, which was also its own place, and when it rained it was like somewhere foreign, somewhere I had been, but had been gone from a long time."

"Why, exactly, are you telling us this?" Her ladies were becoming impatient. She could tell, even though they were polite, sitting quietly, occasionally glancing down to examine their nails.

"Because a home is never a home. To leave the countryside, the familiar. I wanted squalor, noise. It took more than my resistance to the soil to prove this. It took more than my displacement of water."

"Is that when you thought you were drowning?" they asked.

Heat still and the green things. After the move to the place of storms. This was after. And in the world of rattlesnakes there are legends which are coiled and ready to strike. It came down to the valley. (No way out in wading, swept out in a careful wave, all the neighbors waving their hands, trapped too in storming.) How do you learn the concern of trespass. Heat still and green and dying. Everything living and dying. I was there. Willows and wrens and minnows. Cradled in the crook.

It came from far away, as scheduled, and then left in a stream of debris and ice. Most of her life was spent looking forward to when she would see its dark and frozen body. It was the 76th year. The year it would come again. She was ready. She was impatient with the loudness of living among a very quiet family. The comet came when she was impatient to leave.

Before, she was content with small tasks. School assignments or treks to the meadow. She would eat lunch there. Vienna sausages, packets of Saltines, hard-boiled eggs with paper squares filled with salt and pepper. After, she would sit and pretend she was a pioneer.

She did not have anything to wait for, but now there was a comet. It was an event she felt she had been preparing for her whole life. She knew about the astronomer, how he first discovered the orbital period of the comet in the 1700s, and that soon she would see the same thing he saw.

She knew comets had been feared. One appeared shortly after the death of Julius Caesar. One was thought to signify the fall of Jerusalem. One appeared around the time Mount Vesuvius erupted, signaling the last days of Pompeii. One appeared when the Black Plague struck London. One was blamed for starting the American Civil War. She did not fear them. She hoped this one would signal some sort of change for her, but she didn't know what that change would be.

The day came. The forecast was clear. She went to the meadow.

The sky was clear and there were hundreds of stars. She stared at them until they blended together making an illuminated swirl that made her so dizzy she had to look away. She felt it, then. The comet, the streak of light across the sky, the trail of dust and ice, had passed. She looked up and saw the remnants of its arc, or she saw the blur of stars she had seen before, or she saw the stars, or the comet, or she saw the comet, or the stars, or she was dizzy with looking, or she was waiting, or she looked again to see the comet, or she looked again to the stars, or she saw something out there that night, or she would have to wait many years to be sure.

Thousands of insects, thousands of wings. They arranged themselves into a grid pattern. They hold themselves there. So many. Everything else is drawn off course by a huge magnet except for the insects and the shadow walking through the house. We see each other but cannot speak.

The first time she sees a ghost she is a child. It is summer and she is riding her bike down the long road. It is hot. The air is unsteady, like a storm is about to begin.

When she saw the ghost it was like seeing a real person except it was like no person she had ever seen. This first ghost was just like anyone else. It wasn't transparent. It didn't float. It wasn't like the ghosts she would make from tissues and hang around the house during Halloween. It wasn't like the ghosts in movies that only come out at night and haunt things. It was the middle of the day in the hot sun and it was a solid man.

He wore a military uniform and carried a gun. His face was shiny from the heat. He looked at her but she could tell that he didn't see her. She stared back at him. Her hands were sweaty on her handlebars. She felt dusty.

She realized, perhaps that very day, that she had not seen a man but a ghost. She thinks about this ghost a lot. It was the first ghost she saw.

She is asleep. It is spring. Open windows and a cool breeze. It's early morning when she thinks she feels a hand on her forehead. She opens her eyes and sees a flash of bright red hair, then nothing. She thinks it is just the end of a dream. She falls again into sleep. Later, she feels a cool hand on her forehead again and wakes. This time she sees three ladies with bare feet and long nightgowns standing in the corner of the room. They sway slightly, like tree boughs. They have beautiful eyes.

If I am here, submerged, I am also there, in the house with my ladies. I am her, wearing a red dress. They are amusing me with their stories of the morning. After shoving a cup of tea into my hand, they stand before me in a line reciting and describing everything they heard and saw on their morning walk. They tell me a man paced the sidewalk outside the post office and screamed over and over, "It's happening right now!" Near the river, the insects buzzed, they say. They say they looked deep into the river and thought they could see a small pair of eyes. They say the mayflies are getting ready to hatch and they say they could see one of them in the midst of her preparations for flight.

The river continues. It is both still and in motion. The bottom of the river is mud. The mud is difficult to stand upon. When it was warm, she bought smoked carp from a smoke shack near the river and ate its greasy, polluted flesh. After, she washed her hands in the muddy river. It was full of hands and legs, bodies swimming, avoiding the currents. Farther downstream it was easy to get caught off-guard and be swept away. There were so many stories of disappearances.

She has a dream where she lives in an apartment building across the street from an ornate mansion. There are several black metal mailboxes affixed near the front door. This place did not exist before this moment but it has been there for years. She finds herself in a kitchen, all white and glass. She is at the edge of the woods and there is a huge smoking cauldron. She crosses the stream near the mansion several times to investigate. Someone is hauling leaves and paper and wood to the cauldron to burn. When she looks inside, there is both water (an ocean) and an empty, black expanse of eternity.

I took my first breath in a room made of metal. Everything echoed and the noise was deafening. I could not believe how loud. When the oxygen hit my lungs it was knife-like. I cried out only once.

I was sifted through various hands and placed on a table. They left me there alone to gather myself slowly. The silence was deafening. I could not believe how quiet. I saw light through a small window and thick gray shapes moved calmly up and down the wall. Occasionally, there was the faint sound of scratching, voices.

I was half in and half out. I was a coin slipping from a pocket. I was enclosed in glass and felt like water. I became aware of the world and hesitated. There was too much.

Later, several sets of eyes were upon me. Beautiful, blinking, all different colors. Flowers were left, stairs descended. I return to this moment over and over. I can still see them and their revolving. I understood their movements, this vortex into which I was pulled.

She sees a ghost in a photograph and realizes it is both a ghost and a dead person—someone who used to be alive but who died, and who is possibly a ghost now.

Ghost: a wisp of fog who opens cupboards or rearranges objects on a table, or makes a loud racket upstairs, who makes an appearance in photographs as mist or shrouded figure who hovers about the heads of people who are alive, but now, who are probably dead too. It depends on the year of the photograph and also if the photographer was playing a trick with the film or developing or both. A hoax, they used to call these "spirit photos," but even when people knew it was a trick they still believed. And why shouldn't they, and why wouldn't it be possible that it was recorded on film, even though they couldn't see the apparition with their own eyes, out in the real world with all of its problems. Who is to say what's a trick and what isn't and that a mist or bright light isn't something.

She once took a picture of an above-ground tomb. When she developed the photograph, she saw an intense light radiating from the tomb even though it was a cloudy day. She didn't know what to think but she understood it was probably a spirit. She liked thinking about the sensitivity of film, of light, of the shutter closing so precisely at the exact moment.

A line of light lingers on the wall and makes a shadow that startles me when I walk into the room. It is there and then gone.

"Who is it? Is it you?"

This happens nearly every day. Every time I am startled.

My ladies hold their fingers to the sides of my head. They try to sneak up on me. It's no use. Until something is right in front of my eyes, I cannot see it.

Pennies and buttons. Alone in the city. Nothing wandered back. Between the no-one-appeared and the what-did-not-fit, she slipped into cracks. She to the door or downtown and still she turned to the bridge and folded. Her palm buzzed. Her nearly glass and nearly worn and hollow. Pennies went on and off, out into the streets. Once: windows. Her key: something.

One afternoon on the first day of winter, I walked out the door. It was spring, I called out to someone. My ladies came running. It was the hottest day on record and I was on the street. I was crossing over.

The bridge traffic was stopped. Red light, green light, winter light, silence. I returned to my vortex, reverent. I was situated on the riverbank, looking at my wristwatch. It felt useful to keep track. My ladies were there, covered in whispers. I could hear bits of conversation: "But I thought you knew…"

I was pitched forward by a sudden crash, and it was there, on the edge of a gentle submersion, that my mind gave way. It was simple. I looked out over to the other side of the river and was drained of the future.

The river churned its mud below the blue bridge. I was down. It wasn't the motion of flight. There was nothing to get away from. I was there, at the riverbank. I placed my hands in the river.

She has a dream where she is sitting next to someone's sickbed. A lantern lamp twirls pastel light around the room. She cannot see who is lying in the bed. There are too many blankets, all white.

A steady hum persists as she sits. It is almost too loud to bear. It is like metal on metal crossed with electricity. It is like being in a horror movie except there is no blood, no demon, no evil. Everything is white and pure and calm except for the horrible noise. She tries to move the sheets to see who is lying sick in the bed, to see who is going to die soon, but something prevents her from doing so.

She wakes knowing that the person she could not see in the bed was her. She thinks this is a prophecy of her own death and she will probably be dead in the next day or two. This does not happen. It was no prophecy.

A day of sun. There were swallows on the power lines. A kind of warning. Or a good omen. Later, the sky turned green in a sweep of wind. The storm sirens sounded. Terrible wind. She thought she heard the roof crack. She thought she should gather herself and her things.

Everyone walked out to the streets to see what had been strewn. The roof remained intact, but every shingle had been torn off and thrown to the swampy grass. So many people with hands on their heads, so many with hands over their mouths.

After walking through her neighborhood and finding all of the felled trees, she went back to where she lived. There were things to be raked from the lawn. There were things to put away.

The sun shone through the muddy windows, making strange shadows on the walls. She gathered herself slowly, she walked the floor the way a farmer walks his fields. Everything was out of place, as if a smaller wind had come inside. It replaced one thing with another. The plates were where the cups used to be. The shoes were in the bathtub and the soap was on the floor near the door. The books had been double-shelved, a row behind a row. Now the back row lay on the floor, leaving the front row intact. Nothing was missing.

A package tied with twine is thrown off the bridge. A leather satchel full of letters is flung into the river. Shirts, sweaters, hats, gloves are tossed off in fits of joy and fall to the river to be taken away by the current. A handful of paper is sent flying from the bridge walkway. A gold band is taken off and given up to the water below. A woman at night screams down to the water. A man at dawn screams down to the water. The ironwork is formidable in its construction, a barrier of crossbeams. But the river is there below and voices barely audible call out.

She walked along the riverbank and jumped from rock to rock. The landscape there was both smooth and treacherous. Her friends had gone to drive the park road near the river. The road was circular, making the park an island marooned inside concrete and exhaust. She was down near the rip-rap because she hated driving around. Driving was boring and there was nothing else to do but go down to the cool, muddy water and let its damp fingers soak her clothes and skin.

The cars were beginning to disperse for the park curfew. At midnight the city locked the gates to the park so that no one could get inside. She wasn't paying attention to the time and was sitting on a boulder watching the headlights on the bridge that was almost directly above her. A large beetle sauntered on the sand near her feet. She wanted to kick it into the river and watch its legs try to gain ground. She stood and as she did a flashlight beam hit her across the face. Her body twisted around and her foot got caught between the boulder on which she was sitting and another rock. She fell.

The river was in motion at the passing of a motorboat whose driver wasn't paying attention to the no-wake zone near the park. She was dragged into the undertow and tugged out from shore.

She had never learned to swim. She tried to move but breathed water. She tried to open her eyes but was blinded by silt and mud.

When she opened her eyes she was back on shore and covered in the sticky sludge that the river was full of. A bright light shone into her eyes, someone was tugging at her clothes, she heard slow, low voices.

Sad emerald new and lost. The sky broken, I returned. I was a body churning and into moving I shone. It was out of necessity, these practical beliefs, a protection of cold iron, running water, bells, the special power of bread. The statues that preside over the fountains, the ladies of the forests, the secret spirits between the forest and the river. Wrecked and heavy, I return and return and return and return and return.

She has a dream where she is followed by several small snails. At first, she doesn't notice them because they are so small. Their tiny shells barely make a noise when she accidentally steps on one of them. Soon, though, they grow bigger and she cannot help but notice that no matter how fast she walks there is always a large snail, the size of a potato, at her heels. Eventually, these snails become foxes. These foxes are a luminous, solid red. They freeze into statues when she turns to notice them. She does indeed believe, for a while, that they are statues. Solid red foxes frozen in mid-stride, jumping over a fountain, landing on a table, stealing food from a plate. Then she sees one of them blink, and she knows.

The first stage of life equals water. Once she reaches air she is different.

She is not a tree or tall grass or the underside of a bridge. Her wings have always been there. She sends the water away. There is a waterway in the distance and she has flown from it.

If dull wings, a predator. There is a search for shelter. The beginning of clasping. Divided eyes that are wings. A body into another body and vulnerable to wind. Time only lasts hours. It is what gives order.

She is considered wings, a single claw, an abdomen, legs. She has others who look like her. In several stages, she articulates motion. She is in water, she is in air, she is no longer.

In the grove on the other side of the river, she lingered near a spread of heavy walnut trees. She shivered in the shade although the sun came through the leaves in sharp fragments. Her ladies followed far behind her, completely unprepared for a walk. They wore black high heels with ankle straps and thin dresses with short sleeves that flapped in the wind. They should have been wearing coats, scarves, and gloves. They laughed as they always did, walking fast in the breeze, pushing each other playfully.

She stopped and stared at one of the ancient trees. It was so old. Who else had walked here when the grove was just a tangle of saplings? Who were those people? She became exhausted at the thought and sat on the dirty ground and made shapes in the dirt with a stick: a spiral, a triangle, a flower, the letters of a name. She was trying to remember something for which she was not present. She wrote a name over and over and over in the dirt. She pictured a person with that name. She felt she could become this person, someone sitting there among young trees, alone in the damp and chill. Someone just like herself but before.

Her ladies had been quietly moving towards her taking tiptoe steps. They were playing a game. Whoever startled her first would run several feet away and then run twice in a large circle. After that, she would jump on one foot until she was caught. The ladies seemed to find it hilarious so they played often. This time they were all "It" and soon, three long index fingers poked her shoulder. They ran away screeching and she was brought out of her trance, a trance that couldn't have worked.

A sheep is slaughtered, a nail is hammered into a hand, several bodies lie still beneath sheets. A young woman is in bed reading. She considers herself a hero of her time, for herself only. She holds her hand out to someone walking past her door, a blur she cannot see.

She is silent, shakes her head no or yes when anyone asks her a question. Each night she dreams the hopeless dream to be. It is summer. She is in the summer house at the seaside. Her ladies bring in fruit, a sandwich, something cold to drink. The windows are open and the wind blows everything around.

She writes a letter, she reads someone else's letters. Another woman is there with her. She is the same. They are the same woman, but only one of them speaks. What follows are several days and nights where the speaking woman tells the silent woman everything about her life. The silent woman remains silent.

What follows is a summer at the sea. They collect shells on the beach, they wade at low tide. They take their breakfast outdoors and gaze long at the soft sun. Her ladies take photographs of each other in their bathing costumes. They lounge and pose on the shiny black rocks that surround the cove where the summer house sits.

The silent woman narrates the past days in her head, makes lists of events. Her hands are folded primly on her lap. There is a photograph of the two women that has fallen to the floor. It is a picture where the two women verge on becoming one woman, but it is incomplete.

In the dream I am in an old mansion with ornate tapestries and tile floors. The mansion is surrounded by heavy iron gates and fences. Someone walks through a space in the fence and disappears. I see this from where I stand at a large window on the top floor. I watch this figure dressed in a military uniform bend low to the ground and go through the fence. I wait for what seems like hours to see whether this man will come back through, but grow impatient and leave the window. I hear running water but I cannot find it nor escape from the sound. I climb up and down the stairs, open every door and look in every room, trying to find where this water sound is coming from. In the middle of a dark room there is a dark stream that rushes through it, and an overgrowth of ivy and ferns. This stream begins at one end of the room, splashes out the window and continues along a gravel pathway that leads away from the mansion and into a beech grove. I leave the house through the window to follow the stream. I follow it as far as I can. In my peripheral vision I see the person in the military uniform walking parallel to me. I lift a hand and call out, but I cannot speak. I wake choking.

Mornings, they come to wake her, eyes dim from a long night of dreaming. They are in nightgowns, barefoot, their long red hair brushed smooth over their shoulders. Three cool hands are placed in turn upon her forehead. They whisper, *Get up now, it's morning.*

Afternoons, they spend time chattering amongst themselves, sewing purple spangles on dresses, or making costumes for an evening amusement. The costumes are elaborate and identical. They only make costumes of insects or nobility: three grasshoppers, three knaves, three queens, three mayflies.

These ladies, as great as cities, gather their private nations and take flight. Arbitresses of east and west, they wander softly. They are of water, of any river or sea.

"Don't you know it's bad luck to compare hands?"

We are sitting on the strand, our legs bare, our sunhats low over our eyes. The woman who looks like me has taken my hand and placed it next to her own to compare. I pull my hand away.

My ladies are there with us. They have begun a game with shells. One makes a pattern in the sand with them and the others have to try to guess what the pattern means. Before they make their guess, they perform a kind of jitterbug. Then they sit down, rather hard, and place a finger to lips, ponder, then look up brightly and give their answer. They don't often guess correctly, it seems, as they usually stomp off with a pout and frown.

The light begins to fade and the clouds roll in and we gather our things. It has been another afternoon that was both pleasant and uncomfortable.

They have heard of the woman who walks the riverbeds, who paces the bridge. Some say they have seen her with other women who wear long flowing gowns. Some say they do not believe she is real, say she's made up, that her feet have never touched solid ground. They say she's a vision, a shade, an appearance, unknowable. Believers are thought to be deluding themselves, wasting their time by the river, but superstitions always arise from truth. The ones who believe are affected. They make pilgrimages to the water. They bring jars in which to put the river. A river of their own to keep them safe. They believe she keeps them safe.

Her emergence into the world was aided by the encouragement of her ancestors, who appeared for the occasion wearing forget-me-nots in their hair and lapels but who remained unnoticed by the parties involved as there were too many other things happening at the same time. For example, her father was busy throwing the dozens of snakes out the window that had appeared out of nowhere.

"So, you thought you were drowning?"

"I couldn't be sure. It was unclear which way was up, how to move, where to go. It was a strange perambulation. I heard some sort of water bird, I saw many gliding along the periphery. There was an undertow; I knew this from what everyone said about moving bodies of water. The currents seemed to me like a train or bus you would wait for and get onto. But of course it wasn't like that. I was seeing all kinds of blue, I was trying to emerge."

"How did you get away?" Her ladies leaned forward. They held their chins in their hands and sat cross-legged on the floor in dresses made from pale chiffon.

"To leave a place is difficult. I understand motion, but am unclear about how to ignite it. Most places are like others. I often feel as if I were somewhere else. As if one city grid were placed on top of another, inserting its atmosphere as well as its architecture. I'm not sure how else to explain it. It's not me that is displaced, but the landscape."

Place a loaf of bread with a quantity of quicksilver within. Place a loaf of bread with a lit candle embedded within it. Place a shirt there. Listen for the change in the sound of the drum beat. Float chips of wood. Wear an earring. Row in a boat with a rooster. Place a straw or bundle of straw. Insert a paper with the name written upon it. Throw a lamb or goat there. Fire a cannon. Ring the bell. You'll hear her voice before a storm: a crier who returns as a bird. Use a fetish of fishbone, wear a ring of coffin nail, wear a ring of seahorse teeth, a fillet of green rushes tied to the calf. Carry a knee bone, a black key. Come into the world at the rising of the Dog Star. To appease, to make sure, throw salt into the river.

I do not know what it is I am waiting for, if I am waiting for anything. It seems I am. I have been here so long. There was a time I was elsewhere, my dwelling a private district of gravel. Solid ground. A frame house. Windows and curtains. Eggs and tea. I appeared alone in the meadow, ran reckless through the prospect. My outlook was extensive and naïve. At night, the river whispered and I was its likely customer. Whichever direction I faced was water. It was inevitable.

If they could see her, they would feel something sharp between the eyes. A bright blue light emanating from what could be her face. If they could see her, they would see a dripping costume of wings. She is covered in mud, surrounded by air. She is surrounded yet invisible. If she is invisible, she hovers and spins and moves towards the river. If she is not invisible, she will walk to the river slowly.

She dreams that she finds herself inside a large white Victorian house where everything is carved from bone. Someone, a servant, keeps filling her glass with very thin mud which she then pours onto the floor and grinds into the carpet with the heel of her shoe. There is a fern in the window covered in tiny mirrors. They do not reflect her face when she looks into them. Outside there is a walnut tree surrounded by tall faceless statues and an elaborate fountain. She sits at the edge of the fountain where she attempts to fill a metal bucket with water using only her fists.

I had been expecting it since birth. This conclusion, the blinding light, the end of movement, everything finished. I knew I was not meant long for this world and so paid particular attention to the inevitability of my demise. Every day, I looked for signs—a variation in bird song, mail delivered to the wrong address, typographical errors in the newspapers. Yet, each day: nothing. I remained alive.

Then the day came. I knew it upon arising. The sun was so bright I could barely lift the curtain. There was a loud hum. I couldn't believe the pain in my head. It was like nothing else. After, I knew I had crossed over. Yet I remained where I was. Standing at the window in my nightgown.

Small bodies. The dock and night. Weeds on the riverbank, casting in. Windshields and other junk stranded on the shore. You couldn't drive into the river, you could only bob softly. Headlights and the lagoon when no one was there. Everything transfixed and the water was motion, veined and transparent, you could take a small boat to the other side and there was something tiny between the nearness. If dark and heavy, if hatched and watching, if you were there, you would see.

There are ghosts in the world she cannot see because they don't belong to her, but she can see them in the photographs she finds and collects in an album. A lot of people take photographs of ghosts, but they don't know this until later when the film is developed.

There is one she especially likes. It doesn't look like a person. It looks like fabric, tulle, something sheer. It is a picture of a veil descending a staircase. It is the most famous picture of a ghost. The picture was taken somewhere in England, where ghost belief is more common than in other places.

In another favorite, a tiny triangle of a small boy's foggy face peers out from a framed portrait of Jesus hanging on a paneled wall behind a family posing for their Christmas portrait. They smile widely. They don't know he's there.

She thinks that taking pictures in graveyards hoping for a picture of a ghost is cheating. She prefers the ghosts who turn up in the background or foreground, who hover off to the side or behind the subject of the photo. Where it seems as though they are too bashful to appear fully, but too lonely not to appear at all.

She wakes feeling ill after a dream in which she eats too many hardboiled eggs at an expensive restaurant. The restaurant was a medieval city, with narrow passageways and cobblestone paths, low arches and thick walls, the smell of eternity and the colored sunlight quivering above the strangest vegetation of church paintings and carved figures she had ever seen. Everything was enclosed and ancient, the inhabitants gliding past her in long brown robes. Angels, saints, dragons, prophets, and devils looked into her eyes as she navigated the narrow streets. Thousands of insects followed her, all in formation. They changed their pattern at each small noise—a cough, a sneeze, some distant music. Near the river, she took off her shoes to put on a pair of tall rubber boots. Almost immediately her shoes were run over by a large street sweeping machine. Upon waking, she tells herself to remember this.

I was a woman scorned. My ladies placed an ancient headdress atop my curls. Mornings I stood by windows, waiting. I understood the movement of planets, comets. All of my gardens were different colors. I kept track of things. Winters, ice fell from the sky making everything slick and shiny. I wandered bareheaded out the door.

I swallowed swords and fire, my body glistening with oil. Webs of taut silk were stretched above me when I slept at night. I investigated my insides and made a hollow place. When the fire and swords came to rest in me, it was calming. To be filled up like that. My ladies dressed me in spangles, they anointed my limbs with perfumes. They watched me perform, their eyes shining, their arms wrapped around each other's waists, swaying.

All of my paupers were bent and shaken, mowing my fields full of glowworms. Pink silk draperies surrounded my throne of mahogany and finch-bone where I waited. I was an important king. There were several ladies who came to call, they brought gifts of olives and once, the tiniest hummingbird buzzing like an angry bee. I made many lists. Each day I arranged my attributes.

I was damp, my hands rough from milking. I was always pouring cream from a red pitcher, its stream steady, the brown basin never filling. The bread I made cooled near the open window when the weather was warm. I worked in a room where paint flaked off the walls like fish scales. All of my ladies tittered when they saw me coming. They hid their pretty eyes in their sleeves. They gathered together near the lake and watched the clouds fall. Then they followed me and watched how I carried their baskets full of goods, my back breaking beneath their heavy load.

So many lines to follow through. So many worlds to understand. A cartographer's work is never done. I render dragons beneath the ocean. I call them by name and hurry them through tides. If you watch me, with my compass and needle, you will see me pausing, taking breaths of deep blue air. My ladies come with tea. They hold up their skirts to avoid the floor covered in pencil shavings. Then they each place a cool hand on my forehead and neck and they tell me to go on.

"I was always drowning. I felt at sea in the desert, in the middle of nowhere. I had nowhere to be. And soon a box was filled and unfilled. And soon another box and another. Then I would be arranging objects in a room again, hoping to be weighed down."

My ladies looked stricken. After a long silence they said, "There are many ways to find your way out of a cove, a cave, a landslide."

"I've set aside the dark, my fear of it. I move ant-like through the terrain. All of the sounds stop and I am alone with the moon. Some landscapes are entirely of my own making."

There is a catastrophe.

She goes to see a fortune-teller who sits inside a cabinet, hunched over and small.

But she has forgotten, while she is waiting to talk to this fortune-teller, that she was supposed to go to a different one. So she leaves this place with the woman in the cabinet and walks the nearly deserted streets among the old warehouses by the river.

The further she walks, however, the more she senses that the information she seeks is with the first fortune-teller. She stands stranded on the sidewalk. Finally, she turns around and heads back. The fortune-teller in the cabinet is waiting.

"I knew you'd come back."

She places a package into her hands. It contains information about her day of birth, but although it is the correct day, it is the wrong month and year.

She is in the parlor, sitting on the hard velvet sofa. Her hands are gloved and folded primly on her lap. She wears a light blue silk dress. It is brand new but too thin for the weather, which is cold and threatening to snow. For the occasion, she has styled her hair in the new way, just like the movie stars wear—short and wavy—and her lips are painted dark red. She is waiting for the photographer to come and take her portrait. He is late. She prepared all morning for this event, making sure every hair was in place, every seam straight, and now she wonders if it was all in vain.

When the photographer finally arrives, he is distracted and rushed. He sets up his camera and tripod in front of her. She thinks it looks like a huge insect. She is not ready when he clicks the shutter. The moment he takes the photo, he accidentally bumps one of the legs of the tripod with his foot. He hopes the image isn't ruined as he doesn't have time to take another. He has one more appointment across town and wants to get back to his shop before the snow starts to fall. He packs up and leaves with barely a word.

She goes upstairs and takes off her dress. She puts on a heavy sweater and wool pants and walks slowly downstairs to make a cup of tea. She wonders how she will look in the photograph, if she will recognize herself.

Should a call from far away be heard through glass. To be struck ringing. A person is a church and heard on the day of prayer. When the body is a ringing sound, someone is expected. A river claims everyone. Human, demon, or a hole. Something needs to be offered. If doomed to float, if fortunate, the brink. The body bright with lies. A light will appear. Drowning as a cure for water. Until she plunged she remained whole. She who has gone there. What it requires.

At the séance, everyone sat at a large mahogany table. No one looked at each other. They were all waiting for the woman who claimed she could communicate with the dead to arrive. They sat with their hands in their laps, their mouths dry, their breath shallow. The idea that they were to summon the dead back into their world was both exhilarating and horrifying. She sat there with everyone else. She thought, *Am I actually here? Is this real life?*

Finally the medium came into the room with a flourish, covered in dark green velvet. Her skirts were of another era. She also seemed to have arrived from another time. After looking at each person at the table with a hard, serious gaze that one could have mistaken for hatred, she sat at the head of the table and thanked everyone for coming.

She asked each person to talk about whom he or she wanted to contact. She asked that everyone go into great detail—to describe all of the outward characteristics of this person—hair color, size of nose, height, weight—as well as the inward characteristics. Did this person spend a lot of time alone? What was his or her demeanor? Boisterous? Shy? Did this person die by his or her own hand? These introductions took hours.

When it was her turn, she felt embarrassed by the outpouring of emotion she had witnessed. Many were there to talk to a long dead husband or wife, a long dead sister or brother, a mother or father, a lover or friend. In each case, the person described someone whom he or she knew well, someone who was missed and mourned. She was not there to contact anyone in particular. She only wanted to see if it were possible to do so. She could not reveal this, so she lied. She described a sister who never lived, but by virtue of her description, was made to be something true, even in her own mind. This sister was frail and kind. She was thin and small. She described this fake sister as her best friend, one to whom she told her darkest secrets, things she never told anyone else. At this point, the medium asked, "Can you reveal one of these secrets, so that we might ask your sister about it when we find her?" She knew she couldn't say no, so she said, "I don't want to go into specifics, but ask her about the drowning."

Another hour passed. Each person's loved one was contacted in turn and spoke through the medium in an odd voice. The room grew darker as the candles began going out one by one. She was the last. She and her fake sister were going to communicate. The medium began her incantation, she swayed back and forth in her chair. Her assistant, a sharp-nosed woman with a severe chignon and steel-gray housedress mopped her brow and offered sips of water and ice chips. This kind of work was clearly more strenuous than she had anticipated.

Finally, the medium became still. Silent. Her voice was that of a young girl—high-pitched and squeaky. A voice she did not know. The spirit of the young girl said, *I am here I am here I am here I am here I am always here I am here I am not leaving I am here*. In her own voice, the medium asked, "Tell us about the drowning." For a moment there was only a low hum in the otherwise silent room. This spirit girl, if she was one, couldn't talk about the drowning because she didn't know about it. The medium began screaming. She would not stop. She continued and continued and would not stop. Everyone at the table became agitated and looked at each other not knowing what to do. Some moved out of their chairs in an effort to help her assistant who was trying to shake the medium out of her trance, "Madame, Madame, come back to us Madame!"

Calmly, as though nothing were happening, she got up from the table and gathered her things. She left quickly and without a sound.

I am driving on a rocky road that cuts through the middle of the island. I drive the old car with caution. It is lush here, green and full of ancient trees. I am driving to the mainland so I can go to the post office—I have several letters to mail. One is from the woman who looks like me. She has written to an old friend. The letter is on top of the stack and is unsealed.

Dear _____,

I'm not sure if I'm coming back. I have been on the island for a while now and it is pleasant— the isolation. It is good to be free from other people, from the business of the city, all the demands, all the unnecessary conversations. I feel as though my whole being has moved back into an elemental state—I am once again hungry for meals, I can sleep easily, I find I can spend hours gazing at a shadow. I have never felt such clear joy. In my old world, I am sure I would be completely unbearable. Please let me know your news and don't forget about me here, surrounded by water.

She awoke in the middle of the night and felt as though she had been submerged in a pool of water. Her face was wet, the pillowcase dripping, the blankets heavy and damp—everything was soaked. She reached to touch her neck and found her hair drenched. It was as if someone had thrown a bucket of water on her. She was confused. But rather than get up, she stayed in the wetness, her dream calling her back under. Before she was waked, she had been dreaming of a long bridge inside a massive mansion. When she returned to the dream the bridge was gone and only the scaffolding was left in its place. Nothing could pass over this bridge, although everyone continued to try, which resulted in everyone plummeting to the ground several feet below. When she woke in the morning, she was completely dry. There was no trace of water anywhere.

A ghost recovers itself, gathers its veil, its frost and fog, and descends the staircase and goes to wait in the car. It had been left sprawled on the floor, left to consider monuments, the monumental. It had been left outside the vortex and next to the wall. What could house this thing—with its variable temperatures, its moist and heavy movements? It clings to its nearest possession, hoping to descend into a vase like a genie. The days of horse-drawn carriages and finger bowls and calling cards and dressing gowns and forget-me-nots and that particular haze that used to cling to the city were over now. This past was gathered, warped, and straightened. It was ready to move on.

The floor is spread with hundreds of old photographs and picture postcards. These pictures have no order and most of them depict things I was not alive to know. The house in this one is no longer standing. The woman in this one has been forgotten. The man in this one has a nose I've seen before. There are so many postcards, hello-how-are-you-wish-you-were-here from the Trempealeau Hotel, from Winnipeg, from Milwaukee, Miami, Las Vegas, from Red Wing, St. Paul. Greetings from Lake Itasca, Greetings from Duluth. Greetings from New Orleans, Greetings from St. Louis. Greetings from Hannibal, Greetings from Lake City. These places still exist, but they are different now. We are all different. There are no clues here that will be of any use to me. All of these pictures are evidence of something else.

In the room there is a large mahogany bed frame and several people stand around it. Their hands are clasped at their waists or their bosoms and all of their brows are furrowed with worry. There is a woman in the bed. A man holds her hand. Another is at her feet. Men and women make a circle around them. They speak in low whispers. They turn to each other and then turn back to the bed. They stand in their suits and skirts, heavy and dark.

The woman in the bed has fallen asleep. The man stands by the window for a moment, hands in pockets, before he begins to pace back and forth. The floorboards creak loudly under his steps. The other man has stood up and grasped the arm of the pacing man. He says something to him and the pacing man brings his hand to his forehead.

The woman on the bed stirs. She reaches her hand toward the men as she calls out.

I am here too. I have seen all of this from where I hover near the chandelier dripping with dusty prisms.

The night is dark and long and I have been trying to sleep for hours. I get up from the bed and walk across the creaking floorboards to the window. I cannot bear to be inside. I exit the house quietly leaving the back door ajar so that the loud click of the latch doesn't sound and wake my ladies. A dim yellow from the streetlight falls across the yard. I sit on the grass in my thin nightgown, the beam of light making the green look poisoned.

I sit there for I don't know how long. I find myself digging. I am digging a hole with my bare hands. It is not difficult. The ground is damp and easy to pull up. I dig all night.

The sun comes up and I wake next to a deep hole and a pile of dirt. The hole is as deep as the length of my arm. The hole is dark and the morning light is weak. I start to go back to the house, but when I reach the door I turn and walk to the hole I made. I peer down into it but can't see anything because it's full of water.

She begins to have dreams in which she can see the future. At first, it is only small events that she foresees: getting up after an evening of rest, riding the bus, walking down the street, picking up the mail—regular things. Later, she begins to dream of bodies of water, of insects, the interaction between a river and something heavy plunged off a bridge, the manner in which a person looks sidelong at her shadow, the manner in which a person passing on the street runs directly into her as if she weren't there, how someone will steal her breakfast, how someone, herself, will have trouble speaking.

She leaves offerings at various locations around town—a smooth river pebble on the banister of the stairs in the library, a handful of sand in the tip jar at the tea room, a folded paper insect left among the grapefruits at the market. She cannot stop doing it. To people in the library, the pebble goes unnoticed, as does the paper insect, which becomes buried among the heavy citrus. To the workers at the tea room, cleaning the sand off their dollars and quarters is an annoyance. They whisper about her when she comes in. They wonder about her life. Who she is. They find it strange that someone would wear a veil in the heat of August, in the cold of January. They see her take the veil off and throw it in the trash. Every day she does this and they wonder, *how many veils does she have?*

After the séance, everyone sat silent at the large mahogany table. No one looked at each other directly, although sharp glances flew around the room. They were all waiting to see if the woman who claimed she could communicate with the dead would come out of her trance. They sat with their hands in their laps, their mouths dry, their breath shallow, their hearts beating quickly. The idea of summoning the dead back into the real world was horrifying. Everyone thought, *Am I actually here? Is this real life?*

She left before finding out what happened to the medium. It was late and dark. Her steps on the sidewalk echoed against glass and concrete. She didn't have a sister. Yet, this sister clearly existed. Exists. The horrible trance in which the medium was stuck was the only one she believed. Everything else that night was a performance.

I can see ghosts. Only some ghosts can see me. Those who can, say things like, "Why are you in my house?" or "Who are you?" or "Get out of my house!" or "Is this real life?" They live in a loop: always climbing the stairs, always walking out the door, always moving from room to room. I suspect they do not question their repetition until they see me—an anomaly, something outside their fated pattern. They become confused, angry. They want to know why things are the way they are. They want information. I never know what to say. I tell them they are dead, but it is hard to say because I am not sure what dead means. If these ghosts can see me and talk to me, they are like anyone else. The only difference between a ghost and a person who is alive is that the ghost must stay where she is. She can try to leave, and sometimes that works, but it is very difficult. Leaving means losing the pattern. Up in a puff of smoke. I have seen this happen. I think I have.

She has been looking at the same photograph for months. It is from a long time ago. It depicts an industrial riverfront—dark brick buildings with small windows, names of businesses painted on the side:

Thos. P. Benton & Son
Mfcs of
ELECTRICAL MACHINERY
SEARCH — LIGHTS
GASOLINE

ENGINES

The perspective is elevated in the photograph and the sky is cloudy and gray. One of the buildings has been torn in half. The front of the building stands, but the back of it shows severe white scraping where the walls were pulled down. The river is separated from the street and buildings only by a narrow strip of grass.

If you were there, you could walk right down to the water, which is dark and faintly rippled from a brisk wind or from a passing barge.

This place no longer exists. The buildings are vessels for no one. She is not sure why someone would have taken this photograph.

She dreams of a fountain. It is in the shape of a woman wearing a long robe. The robe is painted blue and has several silver stars that glisten beneath the water. The water trickles onto the statue's hands and waist. Her hands are outstretched in a benevolent gesture and her gaze is aimed toward the earth. There are hundreds of them, all the same. They float high above the rooftops. Hundreds of them hovering. Identical fountains in the shape of a woman wearing a long fluid robe, floating high in the atmosphere, trickling water.

The weather was terrible and they had to stay indoors all day. It was frightening to stare out the window at the storm. The rain came down in sheets, the sky was dark green, and the thunder was so heavy it knocked the teacups off the table. When the wind threatened to twist itself into a tornado, they went down into the cellar to wait for the gale to pass over.

Her ladies were nonplussed. They had put on all of their rain gear and sat in the tiny round cellar in identical bright yellow slickers, broad-brimmed rain hats, and big black galoshes. As they waited for the storm to end, they shared a cigarette and periodically passed a small bottle of brandy from which they took small sips. They did not speak to or look at her. They sat silent and gazed at the ceiling in an effort to determine whether it was safe to go back upstairs.

After several hours they all fell into an uneasy rest. Their dreams were filled with floods and flickering lights and they woke with their feet sitting in an inch of dirty water. After their initial alarm they climbed the stairs, wavering on each step, and opened the cellar door to a dim morning where no birds sang. The house remained. All the windows were intact, the roof had not been lifted, the trees still stood. It was as if nothing had happened.

She went to the bridge mostly in the evenings, when the lights of the bridge and the headlights of the cars would illuminate the water below—a radiance unachievable in the daytime. She felt heavy and unmovable, observing for hours what seemed impossible: the graceful way the bridge maintained its structure.

Dead fish it was rotting mud and insects and we went walking there nights the impossibility of really being down in it, fish smell, reaching the bottom, dead fish, mud and insects, because the bottom was impossible we went there walking deep with mud whatever night in summer it was down there, something different than in history, a catfish, it never froze but hovered slowly suspended, a slime, scales like armor if you were ancient and submerged yourself in it and called to the past, you couldn't get the smell right, we weren't a part of this it was more than mud that got into everything.

From her room in the tall green apartment building next to the alley, she watches snow fall. There is a small light shining from the top window of the red apartment building across the street from her and a suggestion of movement. Someone there is taking off a coat, a hat, placing a pair of gloves upon the radiator to dry. This person is only a torso and head from where she sits watching on her wide windowsill, sipping steaming broth, her feet enclosed in wool socks, the steam from the broth and her breath making steam on the window. Outside, in the small postage stamp park between the buildings, two people wearing navy blue parkas are running around making patterns in the fresh snow. They yell and chase each other. Several times, one reaches out a hand in an effort to capture the other.

On the day in January when all water is holy, they plunged a heavy anchor adorned with red and white carnations into the river. A man—a priest or minister, I don't know who— stood and spoke. From where I was, I couldn't hear what he was saying. He held his hand up to the sky and faced the half-frozen water. His red and white robe whipped in the winter wind. As the anchor lowered his voice took on the cadence of song. It was rhythmic and slow. It was old and ancient. It seemed familiar.

The crowd dispersed after the anchor disappeared. No one said a word as they moved away from the river. The priest or minister sat on the levee. He had exchanged his robe for a parka, the hood making a fuzzy frame around his face. I watched him sit there in the dark gray day—the clouds heavy, a bitter wind.

I turned to walk home and saw one of the carnations floating near shore. I clambered down to the water's edge and pulled it from the water. I turned to make sure no one saw me. I do not know why I did this.

She has a dream where she is shot by several bullets from a small gun. She can't stop dreaming this dream. She tries to catch the bullets with her hands, but her hands are hooves and the bullets too fast. The bullets lodge deeply into her throat. Every time it is the same. A small gun hovers in her peripheral vision, the bullets are released without a sound, and her hands turn to hooves. No one else is there. There is only the gun. It shoots automatically. The gun shoots on its own. It hovers, it is small. It is the same every time.

The mayflies had hatched. She was walking to the river and saw the bridge coated with their fragile bodies. After the séance. All of their transparent wings, so delicate alone, became opaque in quantity. Under the swarm, she walked unafraid. The mayflies—clinging to the ironwork, the trees, her hair. All of them living and dying.

Once she reached the river it was impossible to see, there were so many insects swarming. She stumbled.

Come down, come down, come down to the river.

It was morning. The sun shone through new leaves. A slight breeze came through the windows and a sparrow sang on the high window ledge. There were people on the street below moving quickly, heading to stores, offices, restaurants. Some of them were sad and lost. Some had just spoken to their mothers, a few had yet to speak.

My ladies were still sleeping. They looked like a collection of old costumes piled up on the bed. They hadn't changed out of their dresses. Layers of emerald and turquoise and aubergine chiffon covered their bodies and obscured their faces. They were peaceful and silent.

In the kitchen, I took out the coffee and things for breakfast. I put them on a tray. Through the window above the sink I could see the river. It glinted and shone. A barge was making its way slowly south. A few people had gone to sit on the benches on the riverbank. No one was in the water.

I stood and stared. I was full of silt, churning, moving beneath a bridge, the sky was so bright, blue and full of clouds, I could see all the way to the bottom, it was suddenly clear I was moving towards the bottom—a heavy body sinking, my wings caught and broken.

I am given a bouquet of peacock feathers and must carry them on my journey through mud. I am worried the feathers will be ruined—I can't possibly keep them in their perfect state while walking such a long way. As I walk, they seem to become smaller, less grand, more like wet seaweed than feathers, and I keep them damp as if they were cut flowers. By the time I reach the end of the mud, the feathers are ruined.

She goes to the library. She wants to find out more about what she has seen or thinks she has seen.

She pulls several volumes from the stacks—a book titled *Ghosts* seems promising. She turns to the first page and reads:

> *A ghost can be many things and take many forms.*

She puts the book back. She wants a different kind of information.

They are there in the photograph. They hover behind me in a semi-circle, their bodies draped in cloaks. They gaze down at me sitting stiff in my best dress. I cannot see their faces but I know who they are. I know who I am too. I am there in that photograph. I stand here at the window, holding the picture up to the light.

On the day it was taken it was hot, humid, and stormy. I was uncomfortable in the dress. The dark gray wool stuck to my skin and the high neck was damp with sweat, but it was the only dress I had that would photograph well. You cannot see my discomfort. I am unaware of the three women hovering behind me, looking down with grave concern. I stare straight into the camera. I keep still as I've been told. Then the brightest light I've ever seen and then a moment of utter blindness and then the bright light again each time I blinked.

This day is like the day that picture was taken. The sky hangs low. Dark gray light. A rivulet of sweat runs down my neck and I stand at the window hoping for a cool breeze. I turn around and as I do I know my ladies will be standing behind me, their summer dresses clinging to their legs, their wavy hair plastered to their foreheads. They will stand there silently and I will turn and say, "There you are! I was wondering where you were—Why don't we go outside? It's bound to be cooler out there. Let's see if we can get caught in the rain!"

There was light and she was drawn to it. She slipped away and circled a beam. It is the same every time: she closes her eyes and counts to one hundred, there is a great and heavy vibration, and she emerges from below transformed. She cannot stop it from happening. No one can.

When she came back from the séance, her ladies were waiting for her at the door. They stood there blocking her way with arms akimbo and stern stares. They were silent until she tried to make her way through to get inside the small apartment with its bottle-green walls and pale furniture.

"Where have you been?"

"Just out. I went for a walk."

"But you've been somewhere else, too."

"I went to the river and stayed for a while. It's a beautiful evening, warm, not too muggy. There were more bugs than I expected…"

"You went to see that medium, didn't you?"

"What are you talking about?"

"Don't lie. We know about that girl."

"What girl?"

"The one who drowned. We know you tried to contact her."

Her ladies were ruffled hens, their hair was a mess, all the shiny curls going every which way, their thin crepe-de-Chine wrappers pulled tightly across their bodies. Their feet were bare and looked cold. How long had they been waiting? How long had she been gone?

"I don't even know who this girl is! I made her up! I just wanted to see if it were really possible to contact the dead, so I played a trick. I don't know why. I don't even know how I got there!"

Her ladies spoke severely in unison, "We don't believe you."

"No! I don't know her! How could you? She's a lie!"

"Of course we know her. We always have, just as we've always known you. Don't you remember? Try to remember now."

It is early. It is late. I have to find my way home.

They are dragging the river again. Everyone stands on the banks, watching and waiting. It is excruciating—waiting for the lost to be found. Secretly, everyone hopes that the lost stay lost. They do not want to see the face bloated, the skin green and gray, they do not want to see what the river has taken and left. It is horrifying, the transformation. The implements used to retrieve the drowned. The noise, the spectacle. There is a marked contrast between the noise created to find someone who has drowned and the relative quiet that occurs when drowning.

I sifted sand through my fingers and sat silent. Like anyone, I stared at the water before me. I was every person there that day. It was overcast and the clouds were heavy. I was drawn to the water but couldn't muster enough energy to wade near shore. I never learned to swim and so I was rarely alone near rivers, oceans, ponds, or seas. I kept safe, kept watch over myself.

I wasn't alone. My ladies wandered in the near distance. I saw them gathering shells into buckets, lifting their skirts to avoid dampening them. Earlier they had somehow managed to make a floating table in the river. They stood playing cards with water up to their waists. The cards were much larger than normal cards. I could see each hand clearly from shore.

I sat staring. A gun shooting blanks. I became this blankness. I felt nothing.

She kept herself dry, her feet moving swiftly around her rooms in which she stayed, counting out crackers onto a plate, counting eggs. When the power went out there was a hum. For a whole day, the low sound inside her head. And all the waters gleamed, the trees waving like seaweed, her hair waving like seaweed. Beneath lakes and rivers the waters intermingled, ethereal, an account of floating past, hands brushing the banks, a return to the world, seized.

In this photograph, a woman sits in a pale dress on a dark sofa. Her hands are gloved and her hair short and wavy. She does not look directly into the camera and her expression is distracted, as if she wasn't ready for the picture to be taken. On the left side of the photo, there are three white streaks that some say are ghosts. They say they can see faint faces. They say this even when they've been told that it is probably a mistake, that the photographer most likely jarred the camera at the same time he released the shutter. But he did not discard the negative as an error. He may have thought that the streaks were ghosts, too.

"Don't you remember? Try to remember now."

She felt her face turn pale, her body heavy. She nearly fainted.
It was hard to remember. It was another kind of thinking.

Her ladies led her inside and sat her down upon the sofa.
They held her hands and stroked her forehead.

"Do you remember?"

"No, I don't. Nothing."

She sat surrounded and attempted to let her mind go blank.
She suddenly had a realization.

"Why weren't you there? At the séance?"

"We didn't realize you had gone out. We were napping
upstairs and thought you were downstairs reading. We
didn't know until we awoke what you were doing."

"You can read my mind?"

"No, we can see where you are."

She has a dream where she has to fill Mason jars full of river water and empty them into a large porcelain tub. The tub is far away from shore and she only has two jars. She understands she must empty the entire river into the tub. There will no longer be a river. She is exhausted by the immensity of her task.

It is early and the sun is barely above the horizon. The bare trees are hard webs against the sky and the buildings along the avenues are illuminated strangely. It is early and everything is silent and still. It is like a photograph. Nothing moves.

I walk towards the riverfront. I walk several blocks to get there, my shoes sharp clacking through the streets. I am the only person in this city. No one else exists.

It is necessary to move towards the finish.

In order to scream, you need to be able to breathe. Submersion, turbulent water, undertows. A silent accident silently immersed. In order to scream you need to be able to scream. Someone is drowned by mysterious circumstances. Someone is drowning right now. If she floats she is a witch and dies. If she does not float, she is not a witch and dies. Rip currents, waves, and eddies. Someone is pulled away from shore.

A ghost in a ghost costume climbs out the window. The ghost is going to a party to be among the living. The ghost can only do this in disguise. The ghost can only be in disguise at a costume party.

The ghost leaves the loop of its existence and a great wind howls around her. *I wish it were quieter.* She adjusts the white sheet with which she is covered. She thinks about what she knew of ghosts before she was one. She thinks of illustrations in children's books where figures covered in white sheets grace the sky like long white birds. *I wonder if I can fly,* and jumps up to see if the wind will carry her. It does not.

She walks down the street. Fallen leaves are rotting and hollow pumpkins with faces carved into the sides are rotting. The pumpkins have candles inside them and throw face shapes on the ground. She remembers these things but only remotely. For years she has lived with the same repeated thought. Over and over. She has relived it for years.

She arrives at the party. There are lots of people dancing to loud music. Everyone is there—Marie Antoinette, Henry

VIII, Richard Nixon, Mama Cass. There are many witches and vampires and angels and devils but she is the only ghost.

She stands by the punch bowl watching. They are different than she remembers. Their expressions are a mixture of violence and joy. It is remarkable and frightening. She is frightened. Her ears ring with the music and the laughter. She pours a glass of punch and holds it. She stares into the dark red liquid and feels remote. She should not have come.

"Nice costume," says a man dressed in a gorilla suit. "Nice and cool. I'm burning up in this thing. I don't know what I was thinking." He takes off the gorilla head and sets it next to the punch bowl. She realizes she has forgotten how to respond to a question. She racks her brain. She tries to remember. She says thanks.

They stand in silence for several minutes. The man dressed in the gorilla suit shifts his weight from foot to foot, fans himself with a paper napkin. "Do you want to dance or something?"

She isn't sure what to do. She hesitates.

"Oh, come on!" he says.

"Umm…I don't know."

He grabs the fabric of her sheet and pulls her to the middle of the room. She isn't sure how to dance to this music. After a moment she realizes if she sways a bit, her sheet shifts enough to make it look like she's really moving.

She does not know whether she should go out or stay in. The entire day has revolved around this decision and now the day has gone. Geese flew overhead. The sky stayed bright blue. It was the changing of seasons and it was unsettling.

Yesterday she went walking in an early rain. It was as if she were in a different city. All of the colors were saturated and deep. She got lost in the neighborhood where she lived because everything looked so different. She felt completely displaced, removed from both her body and her surroundings. It was as if she no longer existed. Today, she worries it will happen again.

A few weeks ago, feeling adrift, she began to leave odds and ends at various places. At the bus stop, a stack of pennies, which were immediately strewn to the ground and picked up by a small boy. At the newsstand, a picture postcard depicting an unidentified two-story pale brick house in the middle of a large green lawn at sunrise. She left a small bottle of oil that smelled like ripe figs at the tea room. The corner of her street received a bundle of daisies. She left a small plastic lizard among the lettuce at the grocery store, and a tiny ballerina figurine at the post office counter. Her offerings were off-hand, absent. She was aware of reaching into her pocket or bag, but did not choose the item consciously. No one seemed to see her place these objects at counters or corners or atop a pyramid of apples.

The day has gone. A purple dusk has fallen across the floor beneath the window where she stands transfixed in a long dress. She sways slightly. Her long red hair hangs straight down her back. She has beautiful eyes.

"But I can't remember."

She sat stupidly in a low mustard-colored chair near the window. Her ladies had gone outside for some air. It was a muggy night and the heat of the day was stuck in the walls of the house. She grabbed an ice cube from a glass of water next to her and ran it across her forehead. *Why can't I remember? Are they telling me the truth? Are they lying?*

She suddenly became aware that these ladies, her ladies, could be a figment of her imagination. A hallucination. Made up. It wasn't outside the realm of possibility. She was so often alone. Always alone. But as soon as she thought this, she knew it wasn't true.

The sky came off and she saw swallows. They shone. The place of things. Everything had a now and she walked through it. There were doors. A good omen had been torn through. She was walking. Everything was new; no one thought her out of place. Who would have gathered the neighborhood? Finding everything has come inside. A joke. She saw things, but where? How they were. She went back and walked out. There were things to be.

The motion stopped suddenly and I gasped for air. It was sweeter than expected. Mother was silent and still. She rested only a moment and then walked into the looming white building without assistance.

I was cleaned and wrapped and handed back. We were told to go home.

She placed me in a soft place and sat on the other side of the room. I could see her from where I was. I watched her stretch light between her hands, her thumb and forefinger holding the ends. Her dark dress was illuminated and her face looked strange.

I am tired of this silence. Couldn't we at least talk about the weather? The ocean? That it's too cold today to sit on the beach? I only hear my own voice and it sounds ridiculous. I am sick of the sound of it. Lately, I don't know whether or not I am actually speaking or if I am just thinking. We should go back to the mainland. But I can't stop talking and I hate it. I hate how all of these words sound in the air. And you sit there, staring. I know you can speak, but you won't and I am tired of it. I am so tired I could scream.

Her ladies guided her towards the dark red sofa and pushed her down into it and then went into the kitchen to prepare tea.

They brought out a tray and set it in front of her. They poured a cup of tea and placed it into her hands. She sat and stared. She had no words. She could not swallow or speak. She was glad she was sitting down.

They pulled up three straight-backed wooden chairs and sat in a semi-circle around her. They wore identical pale green housedresses and drew their knees to their chests and rested their chins there. They looked like fauns or nymphs. They seemed altered.

After a few moments, she noticed they were dripping wet. The floor was covered in water below the chairs on which they sat. Had it been raining? Had they come in from the rain?

Outside the sun shone relentlessly. It was almost too bright to bear. She got up from the sofa and pulled the shade.

"Come back and finish your tea. It's getting cold."

But she did not want to sit or drink tea. She stood behind them and crossed her arms.

"I don't understand. Why are you soaked to the skin?"

"We've just come from the river, of course," they said in unison.

The mainland is so busy, full of people and cars and noise. Everyone walks in the same direction, stares her down, expects a response.

She walks and soon finds herself lost. A narrow street near the river she does not remember leads her to a long line of old brown warehouses. One of the warehouses has been torn in half. The front of the building still stands, but the back of it shows severe white scraping where the walls were pulled down and there are piles of bricks and cracked lumber piled up. The river is separated from the street and buildings only by a narrow strip of grass. A line of smoke rises weakly from one of the warehouse chimneys. She walks right down to the water, which is dark and faintly rippled from a passing barge.

It was after midnight when she crawled behind the heavy willow tree. Its trunk was large enough to hide her entire body. She sat there and watched the lagoon slosh over smooth black rocks. She sat in the mud. The tree was completely covered in insects. They hung on the branches like strange breathing leaves.

She soon fell asleep. The water continued its motion, the insects increased their shrill drone. When light shone purple on the horizon, she began to wake. She did not understand where she was or how she got there. She was covered in mud and her hands looked unfamiliar. She could not open her mouth.

From beneath water I see light.

It is morning, there is a chill in the air. They looked all night but gave up after several hours. Soon, another search party will get into their flat-bottomed boat and four men and one woman will glide slowly through the backwaters and lagoon. The woman—young, with long red hair and a white dress—will have a rooster on her lap. They will row and wait for the rooster's crow that tells everyone that they have found me.

But the rooster will not crow today. They are rowing down the wrong river.

I am applying myself to the mornings. At sunrise I wake and run onto the front lawn. The purple light is alarming. It makes the house look so old. Through the dark windows I see them walking in their heavy skirts and somber suits. I hear the low hum of their voices caught in the old brick. Every morning I wait. I apply myself to the morning. I sit patiently. It will happen. One day they will emerge from their history and speak.

"Try to remember…"

She sat on the sofa. Her eyes became heavy. She stared at the portrait of a serious young girl with big eyes in a dark dress and white collar. Something in the girl's lap glowed. The light nearly obscured the girl's face.

Each night she follows the black rocks as if nothing happened. She is both herself and a photograph. She remains these past days in several bodies. Her hands are windows. She studies the picture where someone is walking. Another soft sun. She verges on a blur. No or yes. One woman but many costumes. It is incomplete. Someone asks when she will leave. She will leave each night. They will follow.

Are you here? If you could send me a sign or give notice that you still remain. Something small. Something I can see in the atmosphere.

I am leaving this place. Everything is packed and ready to go. I have managed to trim my belongings down to one large suitcase. I feel light, as if recovered. As if I had been trampled by a herd of horses and the sharpness of the hundreds of hooves on my body has finally faded.

My ladies linger. They aren't ready. I told them over and over that today is the day. They are a swirl of chiffon and sparkles. They haven't spoken to me all week. I am standing at the threshold of their room and I am invisible to them. They are otherwise occupied with their movie star magazines, sharing secret cigarettes, removing curlers from their hair. They laugh and screech at each other.

The window darkens. The window makes me a shadow.

She was so tired. Lately, it was difficult for her to stay awake through a meal or conversation. She found she could sleep through anything and worried about perishing in a house fire, tornado, flood. Some days were entirely lost to her. It was difficult.

Her ladies tried to help through various methods of waking. They flicked cold water onto her face, they shook her shoulders, coughed loudly, yelled "Hey!" inches away from her face, slammed doors and windows. Once they waked her, they tried to keep her occupied with their dance routines and costumes, their singing and reciting, their games of cards and memory.

"Just let me rest, I need to rest," she said. Everything ached. She felt jostled. When she looked in the mirror she couldn't recognize her face. Her features seemed altered.

Her dreams were faint and dark. Everything seemed to take place at night and through a thick fog. She felt as though she were walking through mud.

If you have the sense of someone sitting beside you, or the feeling of someone else nearby as you gaze out the window, if there is comfort in solitude, and if the solitude seems full, if there is the sensation of a cool hand upon your brow while sleeping, if your dreams seem like forgotten events from your life long ago, if there is the question of whether that shadow was something alive, if there is someone walking past who looks familiar, if this person looks into your eyes with knowing but keeps walking, and if a moment passes before your vague recognition of this person, and you suddenly stop in the middle of the sidewalk to contemplate and turn around and look for that familiar face, and if you turn around and the person you think you know has vanished, and if you continue to search for her and actually succeed, then:

A crash of cymbals, a soaring phrase of violins, a low rumble of drums. I made my way quickly down the hallway. I did not glance back once. I was looking for something strong and reliable and found nothing but the edge of winter and concrete, a path that lead down to the water.

The weak morning sun brought no warmth. I felt a headache coming on. I was so tired. It was difficult to walk when I was so tired. I kept my steps and my breath even. I counted one, two, one, two. The wind whipped my hair around my face. I was blinded by hair.

My ladies watched me leave. They stood at the window in their nightclothes, each of them holding a hand to their mouths, holding a hand to their breasts. They seemed not to know if I would come back. I did not know.

Many were taken out. The bodies. Violent shaking. The effort of water to extinguish. The bodies must be cleansed and described. Take them to the nearest house, clean their mouths and noses of mucus and froth with a feather dipped in oil. The whole is procured, is stiff and cold and moved along. Pit of pulsations, pit of agitations. Breathe into these mouths, be very patient. It is necessary to be restored. Air into lungs. A cup of hot brandy. Common salt. A robust remedy is to introduce water back into the lungs of a living person. A drowned person may be a person with the cold of living. Sudden operations and speedy shocks, gently cover with nettles, cover with warm grains. Press down on the chest. Remove what is lodged there.

In the dream I grow smaller and flame-like. Smoke glistens as I walk and decide whether to move through another tunnel. The balustrades where my ladies stand are held up by heavy metal spikes. We are so isolated. No one can remember arriving but we all continue to wait, our arms crossed over our chests, and everything we need is here.

Walk into a photograph. Enter into a real that is no longer. A time of other time. The effort to place yourself there. This is different than the real world.

Someone hands her the glove she's dropped. A flock of geese honk overhead. The traffic light switches green. Things are going forward, every car, every bird, every person, every dog, every gust of wind, every headache, heartache, sadness, every leaf, flower and insect, everything goes forward.

Acknowledgments

Grateful acknowledgment is made to the editors who first published excerpts of this novel (sometimes in very different versions) in *1913: A Journal of Forms, Bombay Gin, Octopus, Sleeping Fish, Tarpaulin Sky, Thuggery & Grace, Trickhouse,* and *Web Conjunctions.*

Enormous gratitude and special thanks to Laura Davenport, Laird Hunt, Bin Ramke, Selah Saterstrom, and Lesley Yalen for their invaluable suggestions and insights as this book went through its many drafts, and for their continued guidance, support, and friendship.

About the Author

Sara Veglahn is the author of three chapbooks, *from The Ladies (a novel excerpt)* (New Herring Press), *Closed Histories* (Noemi Press), and *Another Random Heart* (Letter Machine Editions). She holds an MFA from the University of Massachusetts-Amherst and a PhD from the University of Denver. She currently lives in Denver, Colorado.